This Coloring Book Belongs To:

Color Test Pages

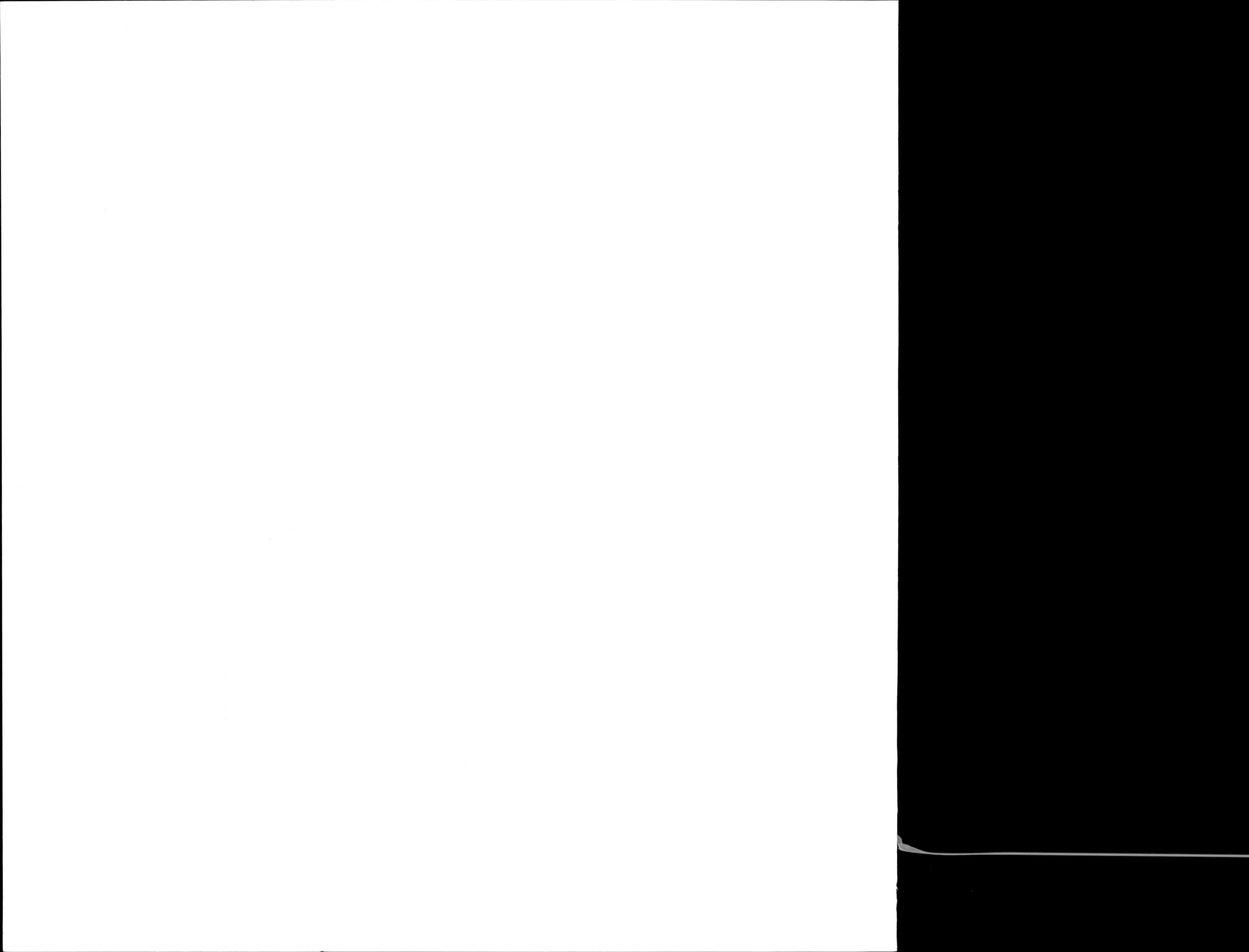

Thank you for your recent purchase!

I hope you found this book is fun and entertaining!
We would really appreciate if you could
leave a positive online review on our
Amazon review section.

Positive energy will come
back to you soon!

LM Clerge

Search LM Clerge on Amazon.com for more books! Thanks!